Finding Sunshine

Written by Shane Nagle
Illustrated by Chantal Stewart

®
sundance™
A Haights Cross Communications ✈® Company

One day, I found a bird with a hurt wing in my backyard.

It didn't fly away when I got close. It didn't make a sound. It just stood there, breathing fast and staring at me.

I knew I had to help it.

I punched holes in a box and found an old, soft blanket. I put water in a small dish and placed it inside the box.

"Come on!" I said. "Hop in now!"

When the bird hopped into the box, I took it to my room. I fed it some honey with a dropper. I kept it warm under my desk lamp.

After school, I bought a mirror and some seed to put in the bird's box. I named the bird Sunshine.

After a few days, Sunshine looked much better.
He folded his sore wing and stood up in his box.
I picked him up and stroked his feathers.

Then he skipped around, chirping, and played
with his mirror. He pecked at the seed.

The next morning, the lid on Sunshine's box was open. I saw him on top of my lamp. He looked at me with one beady eye, chirped for a moment, and then flew off.

I jumped up to close my door, but Sunshine was too fast. He flew out of my room, down the hall, and out the open kitchen window.

After school, I set up his box outside.

I filled up his seed and water dishes and left the lid open. I cleaned his mirror, and I scattered bread crumbs around his box.

Then I sat and waited.

The next day, some other birds came. They ate the seed and drank the water.

The neighbor's cat ate all of the bread crumbs.

"Sunshine has gone back to where he belongs," said Dad. "You can get a pet bird if you want."

But I only wanted Sunshine, so I put out more seed and water and scattered more crumbs.

The next day, some more birds came, and two cats scratched and hissed over the crumbs.

"If you love something, you should let it be free," said Mom. But I wanted Sunshine to come back.

So I put out more seed and water. Then I scattered more crumbs and made a wish.

The next day, there were still more birds and more cat fights, but no Sunshine.

Then I ran out of seed.

A few days later, I was playing outside when I heard a loud chirping.

A flock of birds was sitting on the fence. Sunshine had come back, and he'd brought some friends with him!

I grabbed some bread crumbs, put out my hand, and called, "Sunshine! Sunshine!"

Sunshine landed on my finger.
He looked at me with one beady
eye and flew off.

Around and around the yard the birds
flew, dipping and diving and chirping.

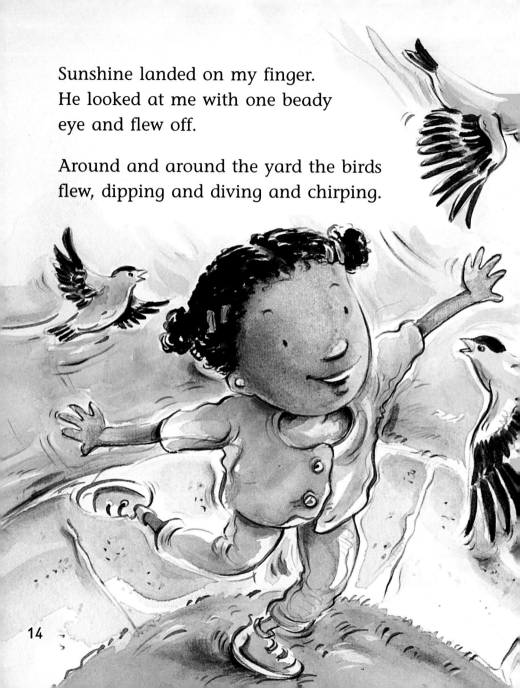

I scattered bread crumbs, bought more seed, and hung Sunshine's mirror in the tree.

Sunshine and his friends returned almost every day. The tree in our backyard was always full of birds.

And before very long, there were even more!